I0779440

Copyright © 2024 by Unity Ink Press LLC, Nevada

All Rights Reserved:

All rights are reserved by Unity Ink Press LLC. No part of this book may be reproduced by any means (mechanical or electronic) without written permission from Unity Ink Press LLC ("the Publisher"), except portions for the purpose of review. The content within this book, including illustrations and accompanying text, is protected by copyright law. Reproduction, distribution, or any form of unauthorized use is prohibited.

ISBN: 979-8-9889846-4-1

Dear Readers,

We are excited to introduce a remarkable new addition to your bookshelf: Discovering Juneteenth: A History of Freedom by Aaron G. Jahi. This beautifully illustrated and thoughtfully written book invites young readers to explore the significant history of Juneteenth, an essential milestone in our nation's journey towards equality.

Discovering Juneteenth is not just a story about the past; it's a conversation about empowerment, pride, and the ongoing struggle for justice. It encourages empathy and understanding, fostering a sense of pride in the progress we've made and inspiring hope for the future we can build together.

Perfect for young historians and families to read together, this book is an excellent resource for learning about the true meaning of freedom and the power of standing united. With its eye-catching illustrations and profound messages, it's sure to engage and enlighten readers of all ages.

We hope that Discovering Juneteenth inspires you as much as it has inspired us. Here's to exploring our past, understanding our present, and empowering our future!

Warmest regards,
Umoja Ink Press

@UmojaInkPress

The Johnson family gathered in Grandma Lorraine's backyard for the annual family reunion. The scent of barbeque filled the air, as pitmasters Fred and Jesse, Grandma Lorraine's sons, competed, each claiming the best recipe.

"Your sauce needs a pinch of paprika, brother!" said Uncle Fred.

"Come on Frederick! I taught you how to barbeque," replied Uncle Jesse, their banter adding to the day's joy.

The children ran around, laughing as they played tag. They darted between the domino and card tables, occasionally stopping to look at the family-tree photos that told the stories of their ancestors. They loved finding faces that looked like them.

Just as Grandma Lorraine was about to share the family history, she was interrupted.

"What's Juneteenth?" asked Malcolm, Grandma Lorraine's eldest great-grandson.

It was always her favorite question of the day. "Malcolm, Juneteenth is about FREEDOM!" exclaimed Grandma Lorraine. "Juneteenth is short for June 19, 1865. It's also called Emancipation Day; the day we celebrate the arrival of the Union Army to Galveston, Texas to enforce the Emancipation Proclamation that freed black people still held in enslavement."

"I don't like talking about slavery," Malcolm said. "It was in the olden days."

"It really wasn't that long ago," his older cousin Angela replied.

"Even though the Civil War had ended, it took the 13th Amendment to be ratified in December 1865 to free enslaved people in all states. That was only 159 years ago. Grandma Lorraine is 87, that's like two of Grandma's lives," Angela explained.

"No one likes talking about slavery Malcolm," said Grandma Lorraine.

"Slavery is part of America's history. Slavery in the United States began in 1619, when our ancestors were taken from Africa and sold in the New World. Our ancestors had no control over their lives; they couldn't decide where to live, what to do, or even if they could marry or have families. Slavery lasted 246 years and that legacy still impacts us today," Grandma Lorraine explained.

"There were a lot of people, black and white, who worked to end slavery. They were called abolitionists. Many of these people believed that slavery was morally wrong and evil. They viewed slavery as a severe violation of human rights, and a sin against humanity," Angela added.

"Harriet Tubman used the Underground Railroad, a series of escape routes and safe houses, to help around 70 enslaved people find freedom," Angela continued.

"Nat Turner led a slave rebellion. He was very religious and believed that enslaved people had the right to claim their freedom," said Ruby, not to be outdone by her twin sister, Angela.

"John Brown, a white abolitionist, led the raid on the Harpers Ferry armory. Sojourner Truth, born into slavery, became a powerful activist for both abolition and women's rights," Ruby said.

"Don't forget about William Lloyd Garrison, he published the weekly 'Liberator' newspaper; and Frederick Douglass wrote about the dehumanization of slavery in his autobiographies," Angela quickly added.

"Girls! This is not a competition of who knows the most," Grandma Lorraine said to her twin granddaughters. "There were a lot of people and events that were important to ending the institution of slavery in America."

"Do you mean Abraham Lincoln?" asked Marcus, Grandma Lorraine's eldest grandson.

"Yes," she replied, "Including Abraham Lincoln who was the 16th President of the United States. He led our country through the Civil War."

"President Lincoln wanted to preserve the Union, but as the Civil War progressed, he recognized the importance of ending slavery to win the war. He issued the Emancipation Proclamation on January 1, 1863, which freed enslaved people in the rebelling states that had seceded from the Union."

"The Emancipation Proclamation affected three and a half million enslaved people. Since most of the Southern states were still in rebellion, slavery continued as usual, but some people got their freedom by escaping their plantations and crossing over the Union lines," Grandma Lorraine explained.

"The surrender of General Lee in April 1865 marked the end of the Civil War, but slavery didn't end in Texas until Major General Granger issued General Order No.3 enforcing the Emancipation Proclamation, two and a half years after the Proclamation was issued by President Lincoln," Grandma Lorraine continued.

"What happened after the Civil War ended?" asked Amari, another of Grandma Lorraine's grandsons.

"After the war ended, there was a period called Reconstruction. The 13th amendment was ratified in December 1865. It formally abolished slavery, except as punishment for crimes," said Grandma Lorraine. She added, "Some people wanted to give black men the right to vote and the same equal rights as white men, while a lot of people wanted to keep things as they were before the Civil War."

"It was a time of change. The 14th Amendment was passed giving citizenship to all who were born in the United States, including people who were formerly enslaved. The 15th Amendment was passed to guarantee the right to vote could not be denied based on race, color or previous condition of servitude," continued Grandma Lorraine.

"Many people in the Northern states did not support slavery but that didn't mean they thought black people should be treated as equals. During Reconstruction, black people couldn't live where they wanted. And they were paid very low wages for their work," Grandma Lorraine explained.

"The convict lease system was created from the 13th Amendment exception. Southern states sent black men to prisons for made up offenses, to work on farms and plantations in return for payment to the state government. State governments were making money to rebuild after losing the Civil War, and plantation owners received cheap labor to plant and harvest their crops," said Grandma Lorraine.

"Yep," Ruby chimed in, "It wasn't just farms and plantations. Black men were sent to mines, factories and forced to build railroad lines and roads. President Franklin D. Roosevelt formally abolished the convict lease system in December 1941."

"That was 76 long years," Amari said.

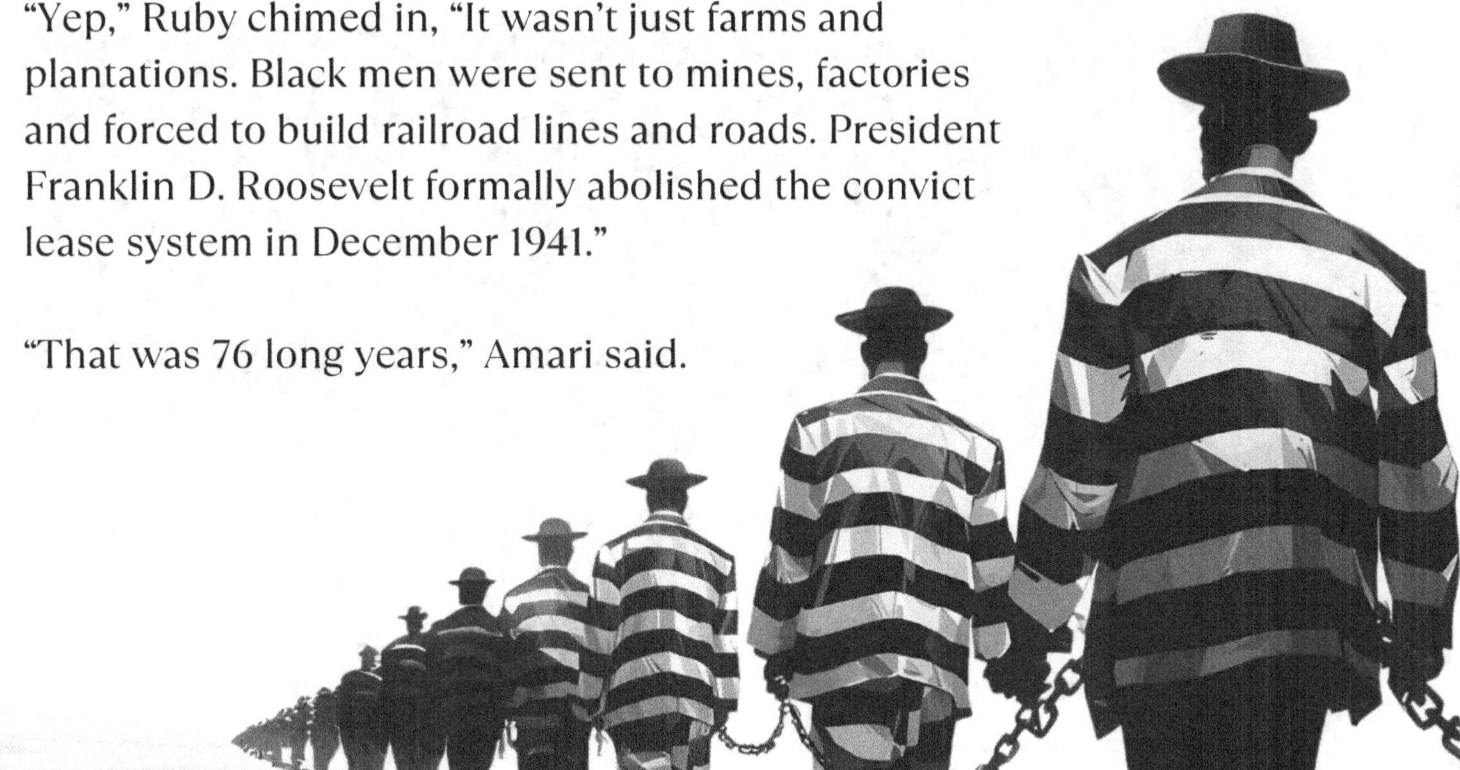

"Freedom didn't mean black people were treated equally," said Marcus.

"Yes, Marcus. It has been a long road, but many people fought to end racial segregation and discrimination. People like Claudette Colvin, A. Philip Randolph, Bayard Rustin and John Lewis were instrumental in the Civil Rights Movement," said Grandma Lorraine.

"Dr. Martin Luther King Jr. gave his famous 'I Have a Dream' speech at the March on Washington on August 28, 1963. More than 250,000 people of all races, came together peacefully to protest racial discrimination and support civil rights legislation," Grandma Lorraine continued.

"Dr. King was the spokesman for nonviolent resistance. He supported boycotts, sit-ins and voter registration drives. Malcolm X, on the other hand, believed that black people should use any means necessary to take control of their own lives."

"The Civil Rights Movement led to the passage of the Civil Rights Act of 1964, which outlawed discrimination based on race, color, religion, sex, or national origin. Also passed was the Voting Rights Act of 1965 that prohibited racial discrimination when exercising the right to vote," said Grandma Lorraine.

"There were other people who worked to advance the rights of black people," said Grandma Lorraine.

"Carter G. Woodson became the 2nd black man, after W.E.B. Du Bois, to obtain a Ph.D. from Harvard University. He pioneered Negro History Week in February 1926. His efforts led to the establishment of Black History Month in 1976," said Marcus.

"Jackie Robinson became the first black man to play in Major League Baseball in April 1947. He was a superb athlete who played under constant threats against him and his family. His uniform number '42' was retired across all major league teams in 1997. He was the first professional athlete in any sport to be so honored," said Angela.

"Barack Obama became the first black man to be President of the United States. He was the 44th President. His administration guided the U.S. economy out of the Great Recession and implemented the Affordable Care Act. Michelle Obama was the first black woman to serve as First Lady. She led initiatives focusing on support for military families and addressed the increase in childhood obesity with the 'Let's Move' programs," said Ruby.

"Oh my," Grandma Lorraine said. "We could be here all day just talking about our great heroes and sheroes, but I think it's time to eat. I want a piece of that red velvet cake."

"But the stories are so good. I want to hear more," said Malcolm.

"Yes they are," said Grandma Lorraine, hugging Malcolm. "Black people in America have been through a lot, but we are strong! We are resilient and we will keep our joy. The people of Galveston, Texas and other cities held a jubilee on June 19, 1866 to celebrate Freedom Day."

"It's important for families and communities to know all of America's history," Grandma Lorraine continued. "Knowing our history is the only way for our nation to continue to move toward justice and equality for all."

"People celebrate Juneteenth in various ways. I've been to parades, cookouts, concerts and political rallies to commemorate Juneteenth," Grandma Lorraine said. "Fortunately we had people like activist Opal Lee and many others who pushed to make June 19th a federal holiday in 2021. Now every American can learn about and celebrate Juneteenth National Independence Day!"

www.ingramcontent.com/pod-product-compliance
Lightning Source LLC
Chambersburg PA
CBHW080603300726

48975CB00010B/2779